Cloud Boy · Niño Nube

Cloud Boy
Niño Nube
Rhode Montijo

Spanish translation by/
Traducido al español por
Teresa Mlawer

LECTORUM
PUBLICATIONS INC.
a subsidiary of Scholastic Inc.
New York

High up in the sky
lived a lonely little cloud boy.

Allá arriba, en el cielo,
vivía un pequeño y solitario niño nube.

One day a butterfly wandered high
into the clouds.

Un día una mariposa voló alto
hasta las nubes.

The lonely little cloud boy felt lucky to see such a beautiful thing, and he thought of the greatest idea.

El pequeño y solitario niño nube se sintió dichoso de ver una cosa tan bella, y tuvo la mejor de las ideas.

He gathered the fluff
from a nearby cloud and
made his own butterfly.

Agarró una esponjosa
nube que pasaba por
allí, y creó con ella su
propia mariposa.

He sent it off for others to see.

Luego la dejó ir para que otros la vieran.

The lonely little cloud
boy looked at the
world below and saw
more wondrous things.

El pequeño y solitario
niño nube miró
al mundo de abajo y
vio otras maravillas.

He looked at the clouds above and
imagined what they could be.

Miró a las nubes de arriba
y se imaginó lo que podrían ser.

He was so inspired.

Estaba muy inspirado.

un conejo

He made big things.

Hizo cosas grandes.

And he made little things.

Hizo cosas pequeñas.

el pes

el elefante

Ombre de nieve

un pajaro

una tartuga

conejo

Soon the sky was filled
with his fluffy creations!

¡Pronto el cielo estuvo
lleno de sus algodonosas
creaciones!

And the little cloud boy
knew that he would
never be lonely again.

Y el pequeño niño nube
supo entonces que nunca
más se sentiría solo.

For Mom and Dad
Para mamá y papá

CLOUD BOY / NIÑO NUBE

Bilingual edition copyright © 2006 by Lectorum Publications, Inc.
Originally published in English under the title CLOUD BOY
Copyright © 2006 by Rhode Montijo

Published by arrangement with
Simon & Schuster Children's Publishing Division, New York.

For information regarding permission, write to Lectorum Publications, Inc.,
557 Broadway, New York, NY 10012.

THIS EDITION TO BE SOLD ONLY IN THE UNITED STATES OF AMERICA AND DEPENDENCIES, PUERTO RICO AND MEXICO.

Book design by Daniel Roode
Translation by Teresa Mlawer
The text for this book is
set in Bookman

Manufactured in China
10 9 8 7 6 5 4 3 2 1
ISBN 1933032065

Library of Congress
Cataloging-in-Publication
data is available.